W9-AFP-413

DISNEY KINGDOMS

BIG THUNDER MOUNTAIN RAILROAD

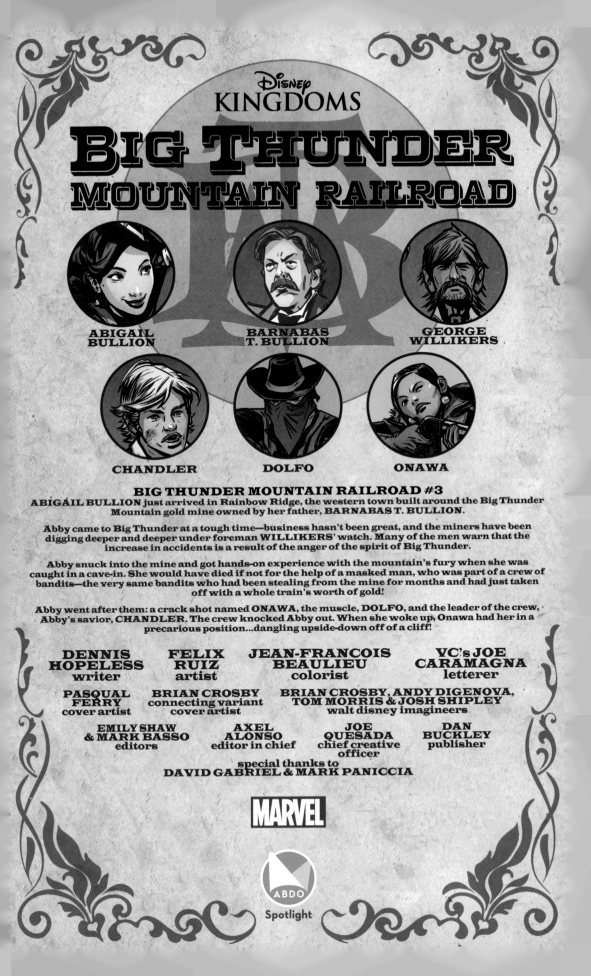

ABIGAIL BULLION

BARNABAS T. BULLION

GEORGE WILLIKERS

CHANDLER

DOLFO

ONAWA

BIG THUNDER MOUNTAIN RAILROAD #3

ABIGAIL BULLION just arrived in Rainbow Ridge, the western town built around the Big Thunder Mountain gold mine owned by her father, BARNABAS T. BULLION.

Abby came to Big Thunder at a tough time—business hasn't been great, and the miners have been digging deeper and deeper under foreman WILLIKERS' watch. Many of the men warn that the increase in accidents is a result of the anger of the spirit of Big Thunder.

Abby snuck into the mine and got hands-on experience with the mountain's fury when she was caught in a cave-in. She would have died if not for the help of a masked man, who was part of a crew of bandits—the very same bandits who had been stealing from the mine for months and had just taken off with a whole train's worth of gold!

Abby went after them: a crack shot named ONAWA, the muscle, DOLFO, and the leader of the crew, Abby's savior, CHANDLER. The crew knocked Abby out. When she woke up, Onawa had her in a precarious position...dangling upside-down off of a cliff!

DENNIS HOPELESS writer

FELIX RUIZ artist

JEAN-FRANCOIS BEAULIEU colorist

VC's JOE CARAMAGNA letterer

PASQUAL FERRY cover artist

BRIAN CROSBY connecting variant cover artist

BRIAN CROSBY, ANDY DIGENOVA, TOM MORRIS & JOSH SHIPLEY walt disney imagineers

EMILY SHAW & MARK BASSO editors

AXEL ALONSO editor in chief

JOE QUESADA chief creative officer

DAN BUCKLEY publisher

special thanks to
DAVID GABRIEL & MARK PANICCIA

MARVEL

ABDO Spotlight

ABDOPUBLISHING.COM

Reinforced library bound edition published in 2017 by Spotlight, a division of ABDO, PO Box 398166, Minneapolis, Minnesota 55439. Spotlight produces high-quality reinforced library bound editions for schools and libraries. Published by agreement with Marvel Characters, Inc.

Printed in the United States of America, North Mankato, Minnesota.
092016
012017

THIS BOOK CONTAINS RECYCLED MATERIALS

MARVEL
marvelkids.com

PUBLISHER'S CATALOGING IN PUBLICATION DATA

Names: Hopeless, Dennis, author. | Walker, Tigh ; Beaulieu, Jean-Francois ; Ruiz, Felix ; Mogorron, Guillermo, illustrators.
Title: Big Thunder Mountain Railroad / writer: Dennis Hopeless ; art: Tigh Walker ; Jean-Francois Beaulieu ; Felix Ruiz ; Guillermo Mogorron.
Description: Reinforced library bound edition. | Minneapolis, Minnesota : Spotlight, 2017. | Series: Disney Kingdoms: Big Thunder Mountain Railroad | Volumes 1, 2 and 4 written by Dennis Hopeless ; illustrated by Tigh Walker & Jean-Francois Beaulieu. | Volume 3 written by Dennis Hopeless ; illustrated by Felix Ruiz & Jean-Francois Beaulieu. | Volume 5 written by Dennis Hopeless ; illustrated by Tigh Walker, Guillermo Mogorron & Jean-Francois Beaulieu.
Summary: When Abby traveled west to Rainbow Ridge to live with her father Barnabas T. Bullion at the Big Thunder Mountain gold mine, the brave young hero never thought she'd join a group of bandits to rob her own father's mine.
Identifiers: LCCN 2016941684 | ISBN 9781614795759 (v.1 ; lib. bdg.) | ISBN 9781614795766 (v.2 ; lib. bdg.) | ISBN 9781614795773 (v.3 ; lib. bdg.) | ISBN 9781614795780 (v.4 ; lib. bdg.) | ISBN 9781614795797 (v.5 ; lib. bdg.)
Subjects: Disney (Fictitious characters)--Juvenile fiction. | Adventures and adventurers--Juvenile fiction. | Graphic novels--Juvenile fiction.
Classification: DDC 741.5--dc23
LC record available at https://lccn.loc.gov/2016941684

ABDO
Spotlight

A Division of ABDO
abdopublishing.com

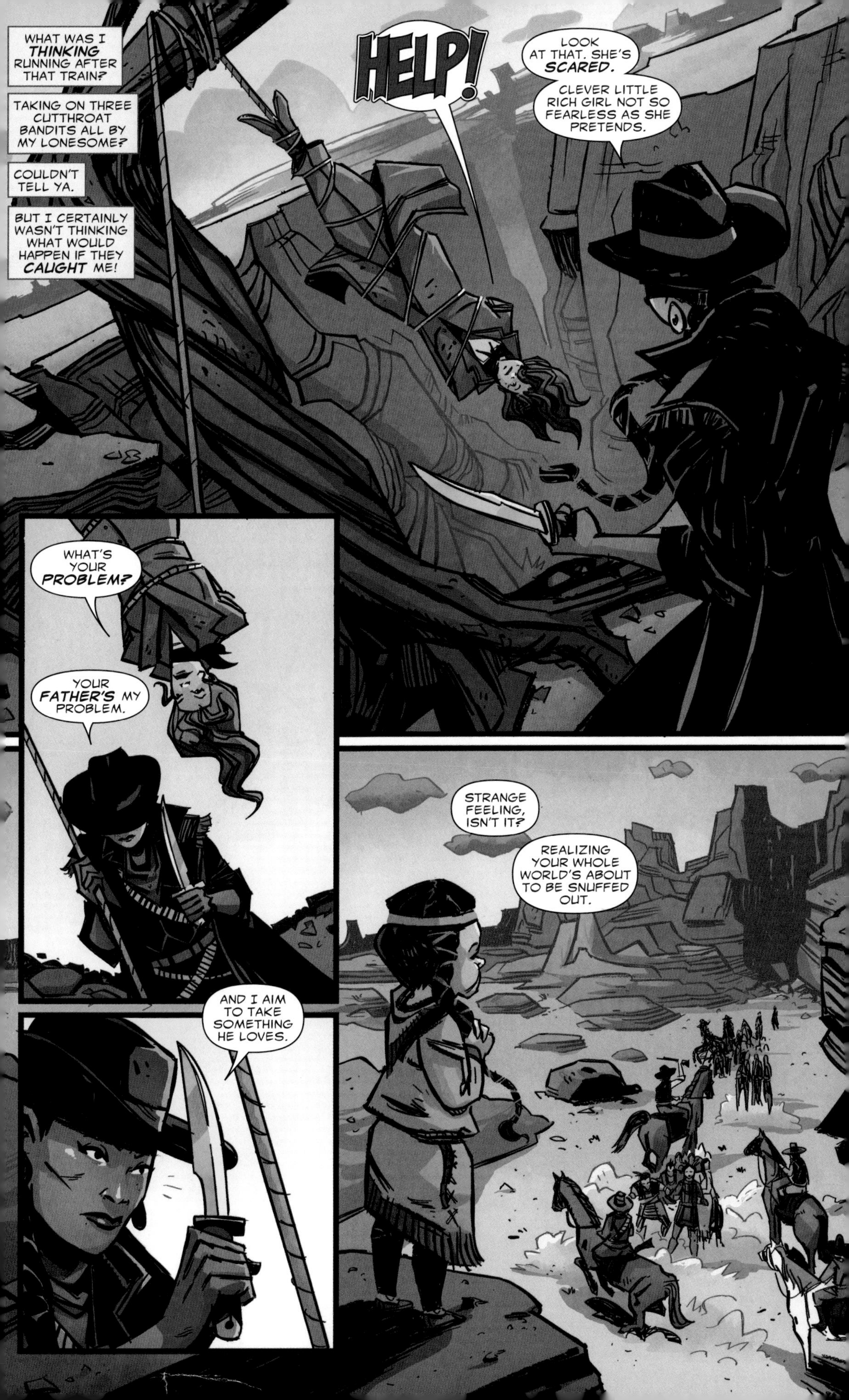
WHAT WAS I THINKING RUNNING AFTER THAT TRAIN?
TAKING ON THREE CUTTHROAT BANDITS ALL BY MY LONESOME?
COULDN'T TELL YA.
BUT I CERTAINLY WASN'T THINKING WHAT WOULD HAPPEN IF THEY CAUGHT ME!
HELP!
LOOK AT THAT. SHE'S SCARED.
CLEVER LITTLE RICH GIRL NOT SO FEARLESS AS SHE PRETENDS.
WHAT'S YOUR PROBLEM?
YOUR FATHER'S MY PROBLEM.
AND I AIM TO TAKE SOMETHING HE LOVES.
STRANGE FEELING, ISN'T IT?
REALIZING YOUR WHOLE WORLD'S ABOUT TO BE SNUFFED OUT.

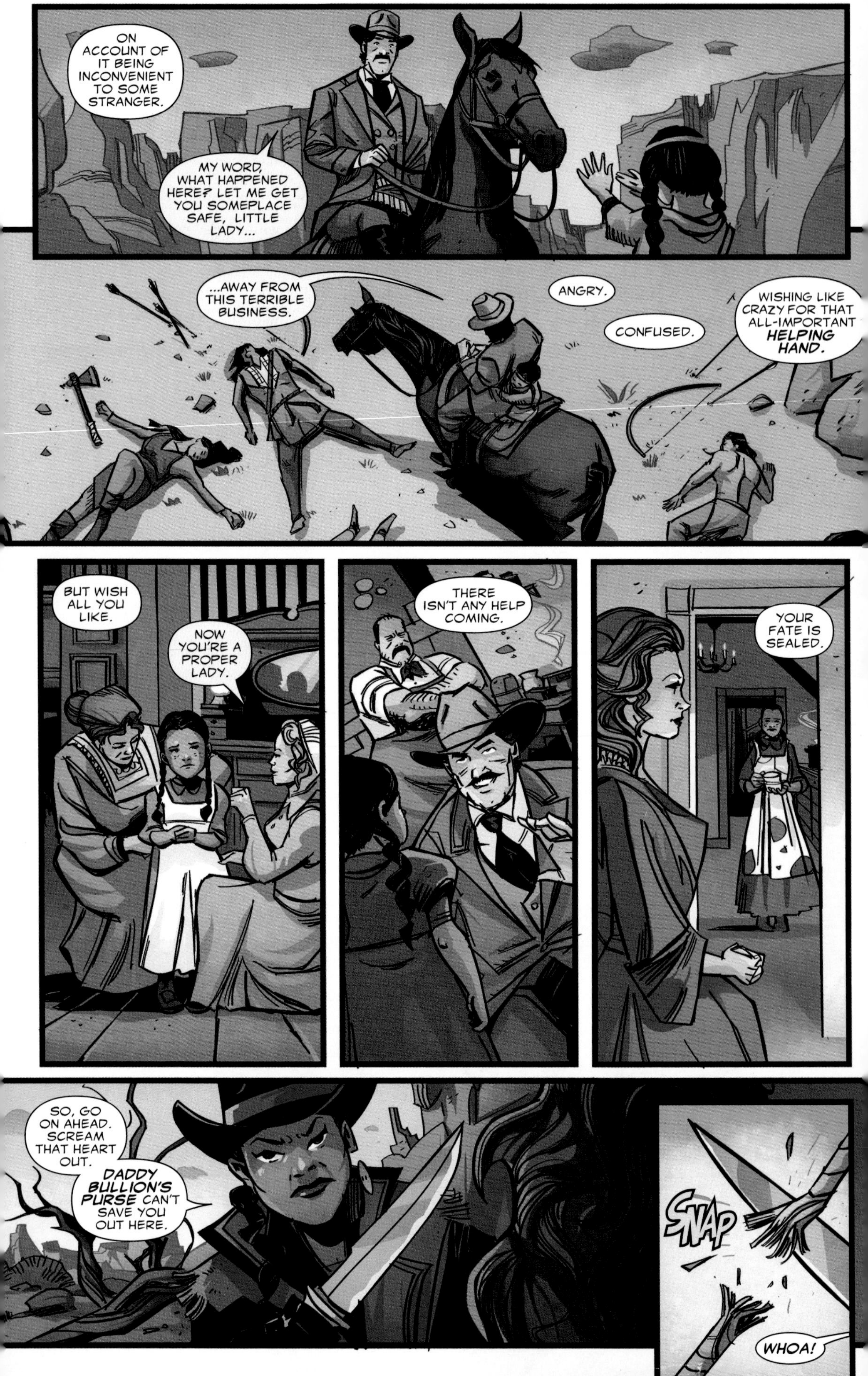
ON ACCOUNT OF IT BEING INCONVENIENT TO SOME STRANGER.
MY WORD, WHAT HAPPENED HERE? LET ME GET YOU SOMEPLACE SAFE, LITTLE LADY...
...AWAY FROM THIS TERRIBLE BUSINESS.
ANGRY.
CONFUSED.
WISHING LIKE CRAZY FOR THAT ALL-IMPORTANT **HELPING HAND.**
BUT WISH ALL YOU LIKE.
NOW YOU'RE A PROPER LADY.
THERE ISN'T ANY HELP COMING.
YOUR FATE IS SEALED.
SO, GO ON AHEAD. SCREAM THAT HEART OUT.
DADDY BULLION'S PURSE CAN'T SAVE YOU OUT HERE.
SNAP
WHOA!

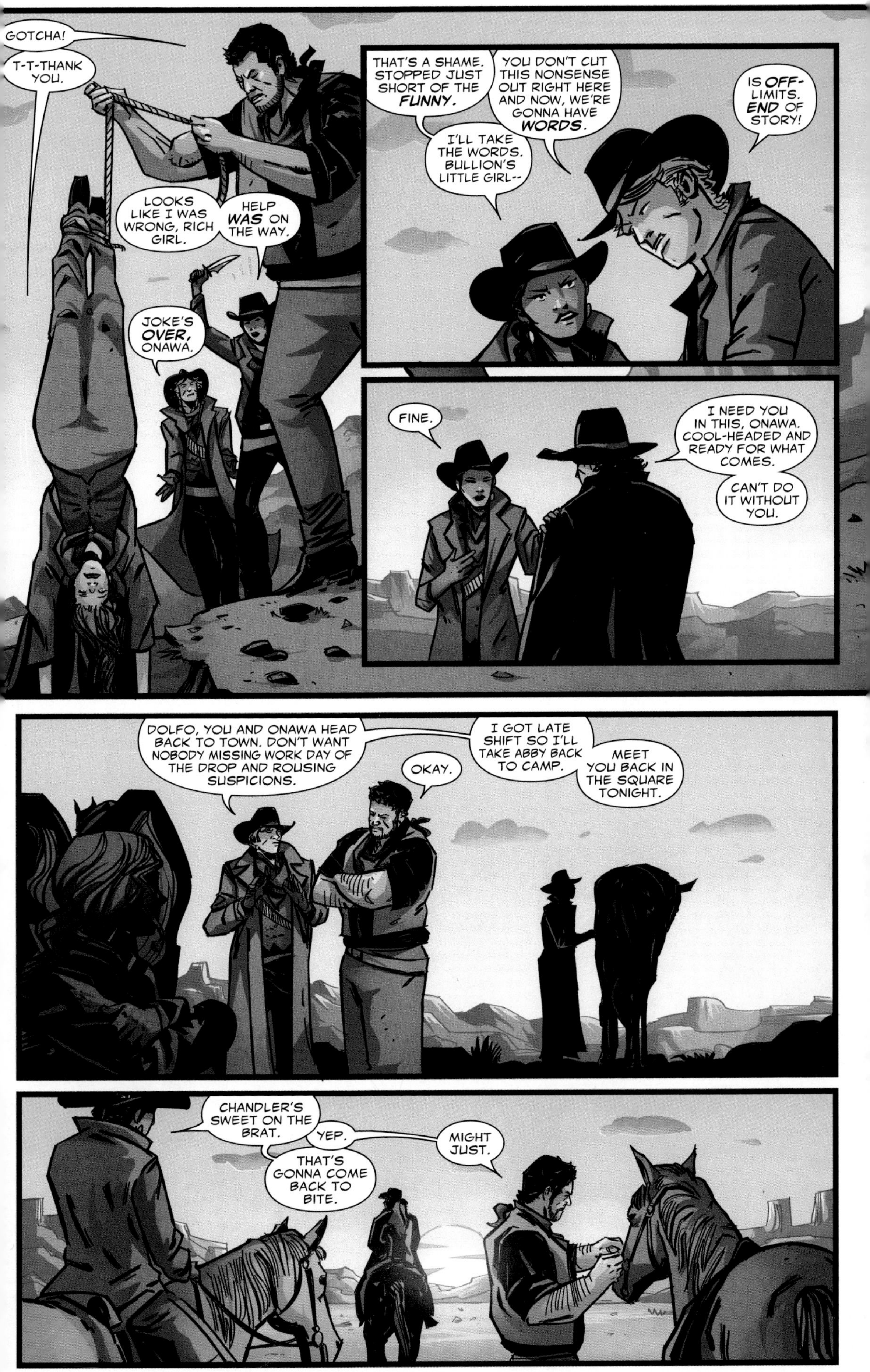
GOTCHA!
T-T-THANK YOU.
LOOKS LIKE I WAS WRONG, RICH GIRL.
HELP WAS ON THE WAY.
JOKE'S OVER, ONAWA.
THAT'S A SHAME. STOPPED JUST SHORT OF THE FUNNY.
YOU DON'T CUT THIS NONSENSE OUT RIGHT HERE AND NOW, WE'RE GONNA HAVE WORDS.
I'LL TAKE THE WORDS. BULLION'S LITTLE GIRL--
IS OFF-LIMITS. END OF STORY!
FINE.
I NEED YOU IN THIS, ONAWA. COOL-HEADED AND READY FOR WHAT COMES.
CAN'T DO IT WITHOUT YOU.
DOLFO, YOU AND ONAWA HEAD BACK TO TOWN. DON'T WANT NOBODY MISSING WORK DAY OF THE DROP AND ROUSING SUSPICIONS.
OKAY.
I GOT LATE SHIFT SO I'LL TAKE ABBY BACK TO CAMP.
MEET YOU BACK IN THE SQUARE TONIGHT.
CHANDLER'S SWEET ON THE BRAT.
YEP.
THAT'S GONNA COME BACK TO BITE.
MIGHT JUST.

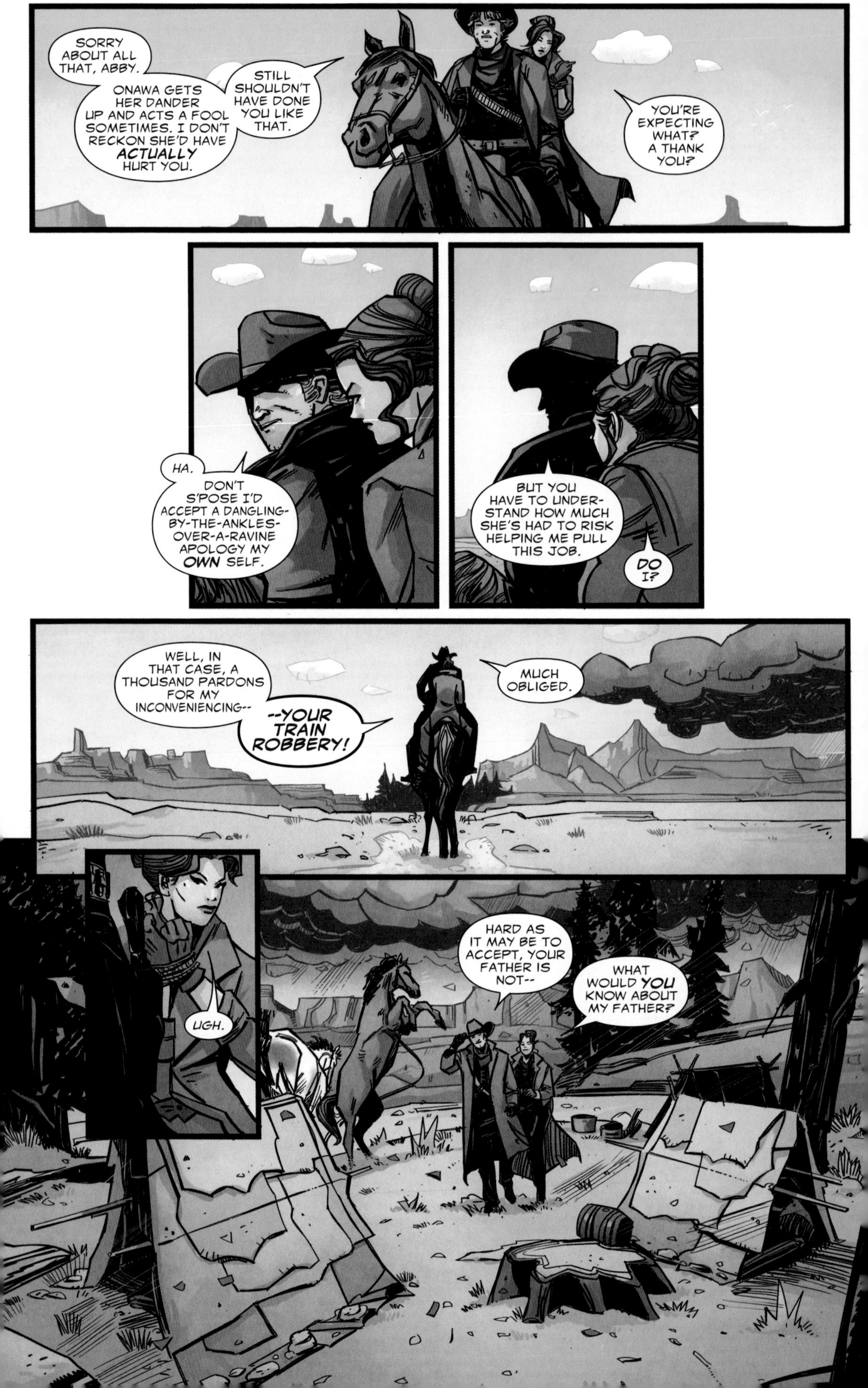

SORRY ABOUT ALL THAT, ABBY.
ONAWA GETS HER DANDER UP AND ACTS A FOOL SOMETIMES. I DON'T RECKON SHE'D HAVE ACTUALLY HURT YOU.
STILL SHOULDN'T HAVE DONE YOU LIKE THAT.
YOU'RE EXPECTING WHAT? A THANK YOU?
HA.
DON'T S'POSE I'D ACCEPT A DANGLING-BY-THE-ANKLES-OVER-A-RAVINE APOLOGY MY OWN SELF.
BUT YOU HAVE TO UNDER-STAND HOW MUCH SHE'S HAD TO RISK HELPING ME PULL THIS JOB.
DO I?
WELL, IN THAT CASE, A THOUSAND PARDONS FOR MY INCONVENIENCING--
--YOUR TRAIN ROBBERY!
MUCH OBLIGED.
UGH.
HARD AS IT MAY BE TO ACCEPT, YOUR FATHER IS NOT--
WHAT WOULD YOU KNOW ABOUT MY FATHER?

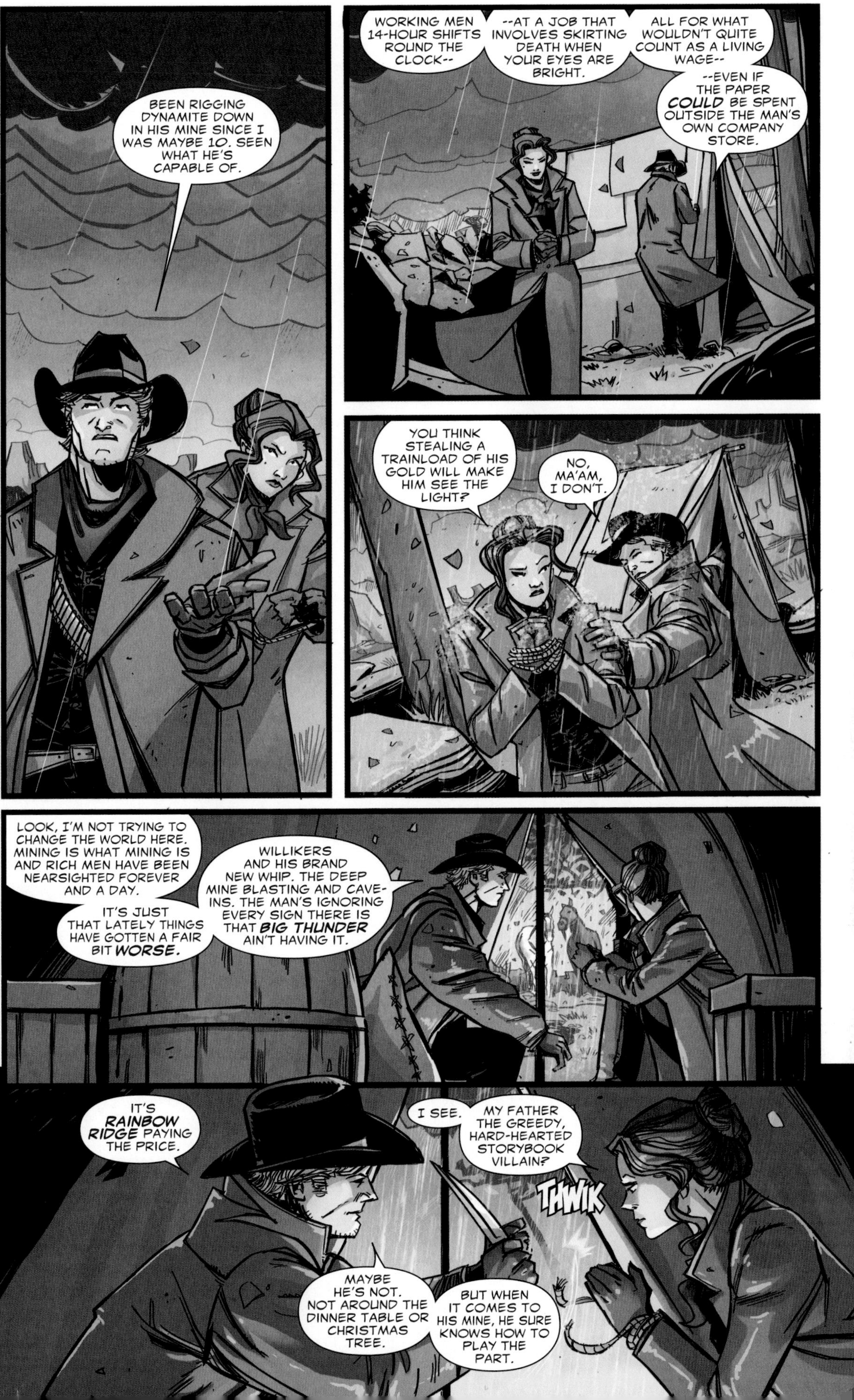
BEEN RIGGING DYNAMITE DOWN IN HIS MINE SINCE I WAS MAYBE 10. SEEN WHAT HE'S CAPABLE OF.
WORKING MEN 14-HOUR SHIFTS ROUND THE CLOCK--
--AT A JOB THAT INVOLVES SKIRTING DEATH WHEN YOUR EYES ARE BRIGHT.
ALL FOR WHAT WOULDN'T QUITE COUNT AS A LIVING WAGE--
--EVEN IF THE PAPER COULD BE SPENT OUTSIDE THE MAN'S OWN COMPANY STORE.
YOU THINK STEALING A TRAINLOAD OF HIS GOLD WILL MAKE HIM SEE THE LIGHT?
NO, MA'AM, I DON'T.
LOOK, I'M NOT TRYING TO CHANGE THE WORLD HERE. MINING IS WHAT MINING IS AND RICH MEN HAVE BEEN NEARSIGHTED FOREVER AND A DAY.
IT'S JUST THAT LATELY THINGS HAVE GOTTEN A FAIR BIT WORSE.
WILLIKERS AND HIS BRAND NEW WHIP. THE DEEP MINE BLASTING AND CAVE-INS. THE MAN'S IGNORING EVERY SIGN THERE IS THAT BIG THUNDER AIN'T HAVING IT.
IT'S RAINBOW RIDGE PAYING THE PRICE.
I SEE.
MY FATHER THE GREEDY, HARD-HEARTED STORYBOOK VILLAIN?
THWIK
MAYBE HE'S NOT. NOT AROUND THE DINNER TABLE OR CHRISTMAS TREE.
BUT WHEN IT COMES TO HIS MINE, HE SURE KNOWS HOW TO PLAY THE PART.

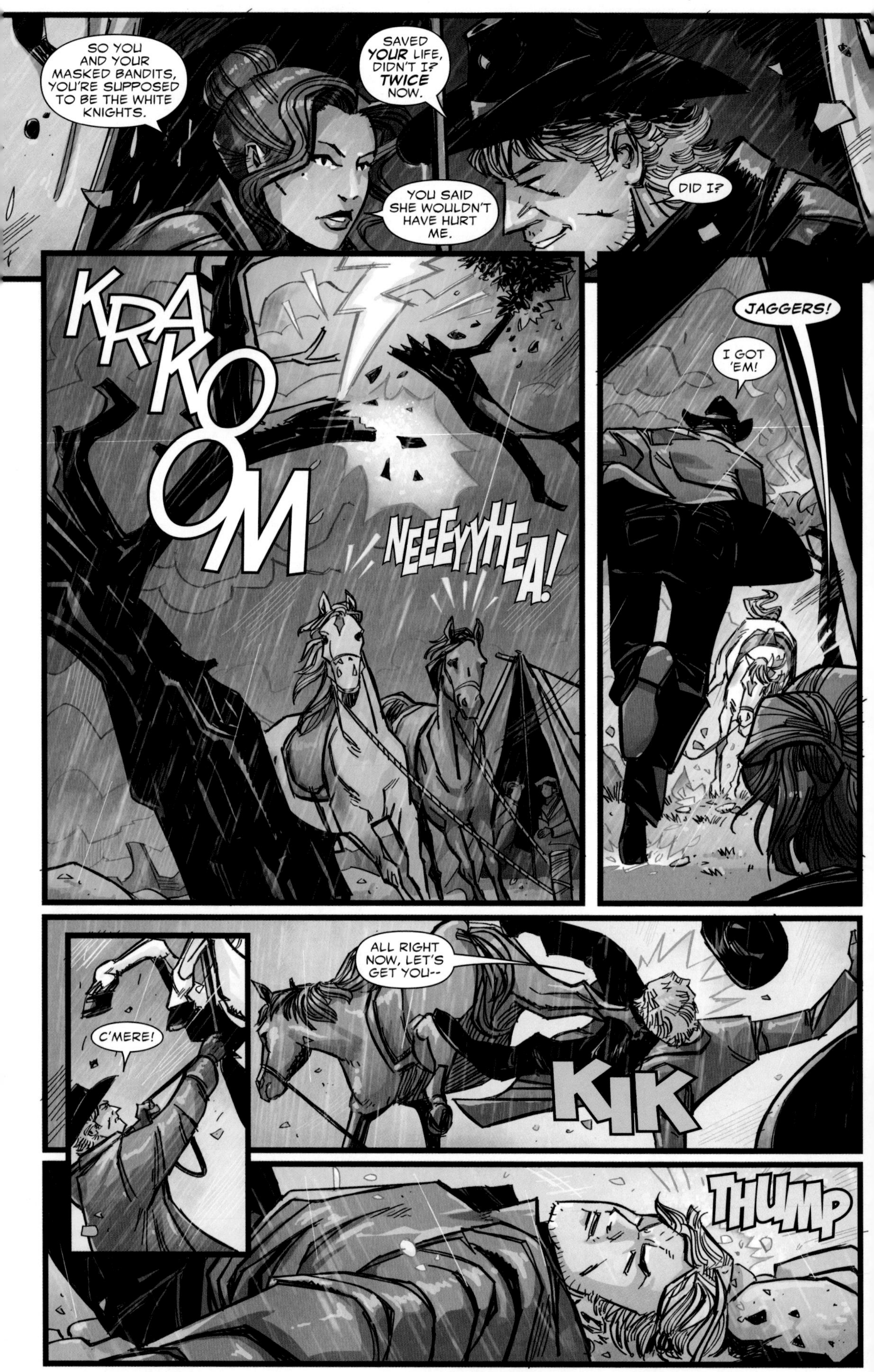
SO YOU AND YOUR MASKED BANDITS, YOU'RE SUPPOSED TO BE THE WHITE KNIGHTS.
SAVED YOUR LIFE, DIDN'T I? TWICE NOW.
YOU SAID SHE WOULDN'T HAVE HURT ME.
DID I?
KRAKOOM
NEEEYYHEA!
JAGGERS!
I GOT 'EM!
ALL RIGHT NOW, LET'S GET YOU--
C'MERE!
KIK
THUMP

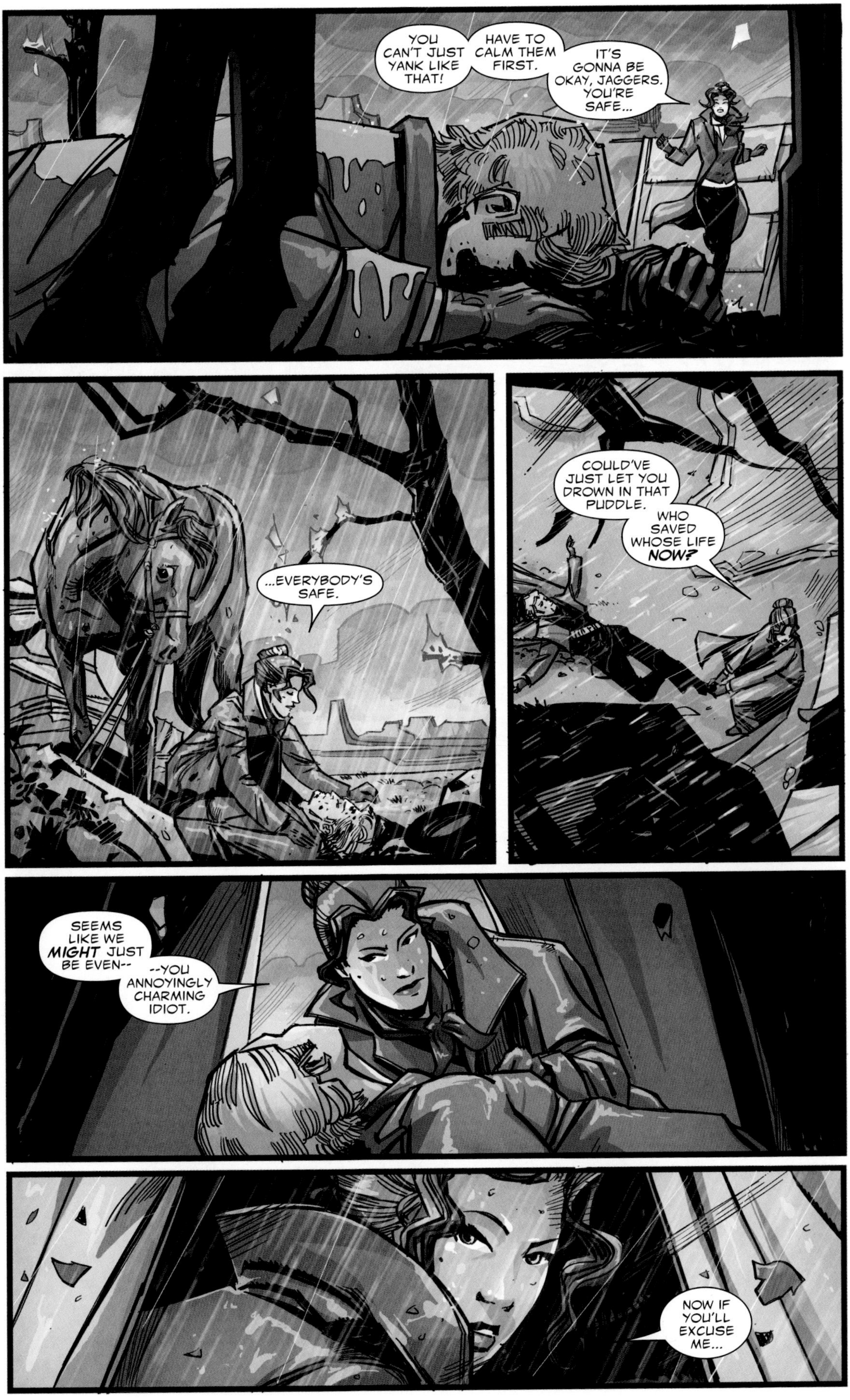
YOU CAN'T JUST YANK LIKE THAT!
HAVE TO CALM THEM FIRST.
IT'S GONNA BE OKAY, JAGGERS. YOU'RE SAFE...
...EVERYBODY'S SAFE.
COULD'VE JUST LET YOU DROWN IN THAT PUDDLE.
WHO SAVED WHOSE LIFE NOW?
SEEMS LIKE WE MIGHT JUST BE EVEN--
--YOU ANNOYINGLY CHARMING IDIOT.
NOW IF YOU'LL EXCUSE ME...

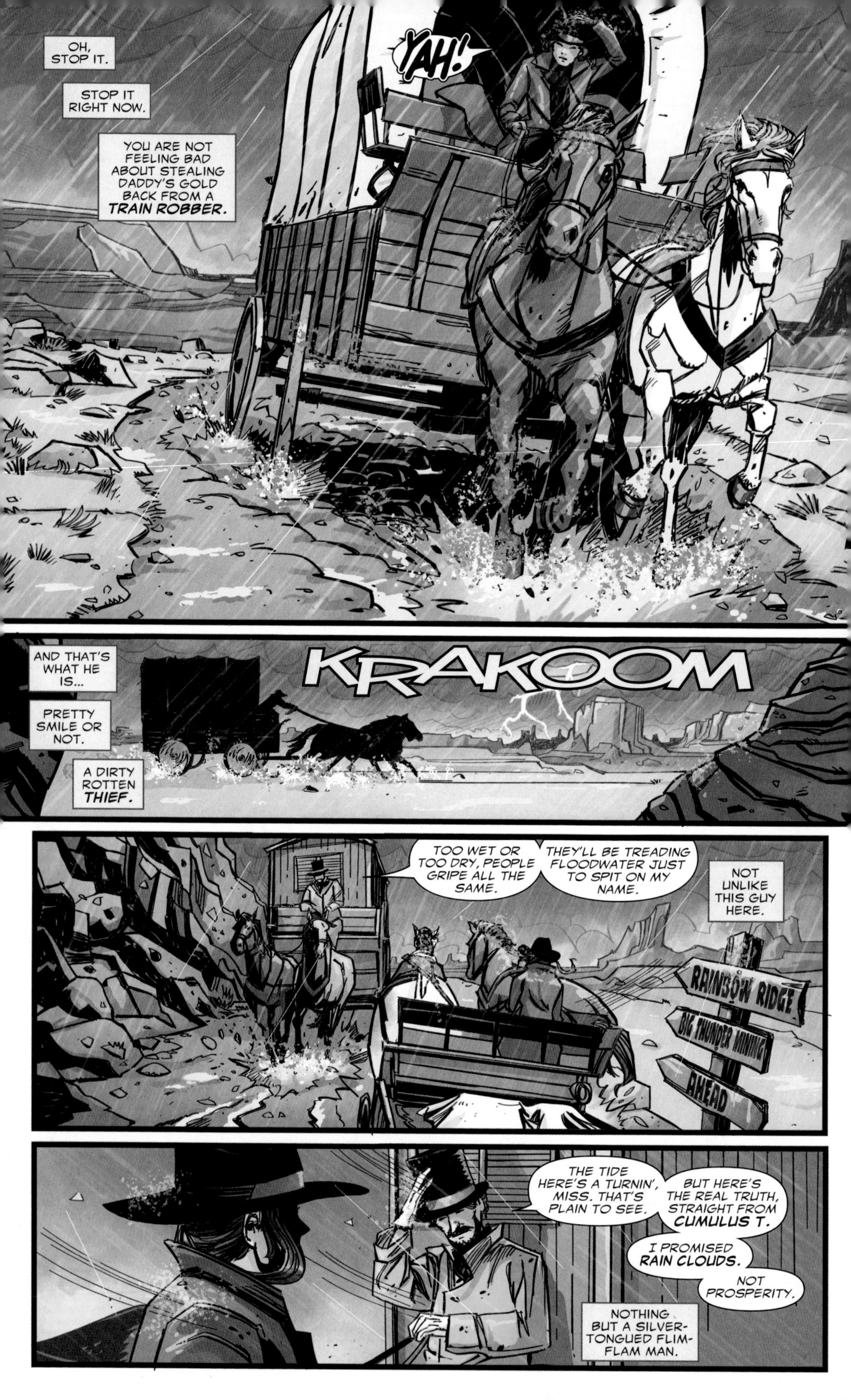
OH, STOP IT.
YAH!
STOP IT RIGHT NOW.
YOU ARE NOT FEELING BAD ABOUT STEALING DADDY'S GOLD BACK FROM A TRAIN ROBBER.
AND THAT'S WHAT HE IS...
KRAKOOM
PRETTY SMILE OR NOT.
A DIRTY ROTTEN THIEF.
TOO WET OR TOO DRY, PEOPLE GRIPE ALL THE SAME.
THEY'LL BE TREADING FLOODWATER JUST TO SPIT ON MY NAME.
NOT UNLIKE THIS GUY HERE.
RAINBOW RIDGE
BIG THUNDER MINING
AHEAD
THE TIDE HERE'S A TURNIN', MISS. THAT'S PLAIN TO SEE.
BUT HERE'S THE REAL TRUTH, STRAIGHT FROM CUMULUS T.
I PROMISED RAIN CLOUDS.
NOT PROSPERITY.
NOTHING BUT A SILVER-TONGUED FLIM-FLAM MAN.

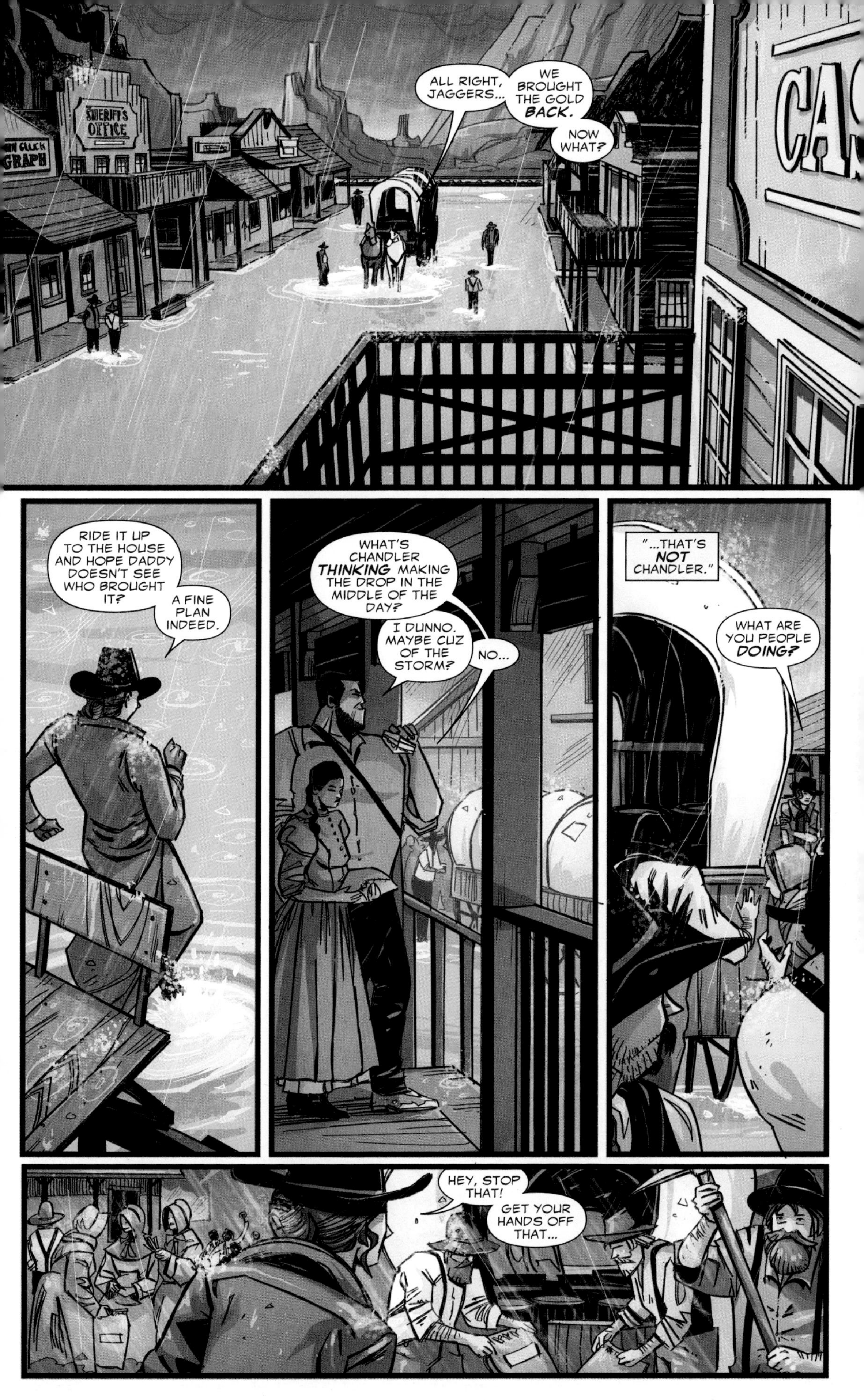
SHERIFF'S OFFICE
GRAPH
ALL RIGHT, JAGGERS...
WE BROUGHT THE GOLD BACK.
NOW WHAT?
RIDE IT UP TO THE HOUSE AND HOPE DADDY DOESN'T SEE WHO BROUGHT IT?
A FINE PLAN INDEED.
WHAT'S CHANDLER THINKING MAKING THE DROP IN THE MIDDLE OF THE DAY?
I DUNNO. MAYBE CUZ OF THE STORM?
NO...
"...THAT'S NOT CHANDLER."
WHAT ARE YOU PEOPLE DOING?
HEY, STOP THAT!
GET YOUR HANDS OFF THAT...

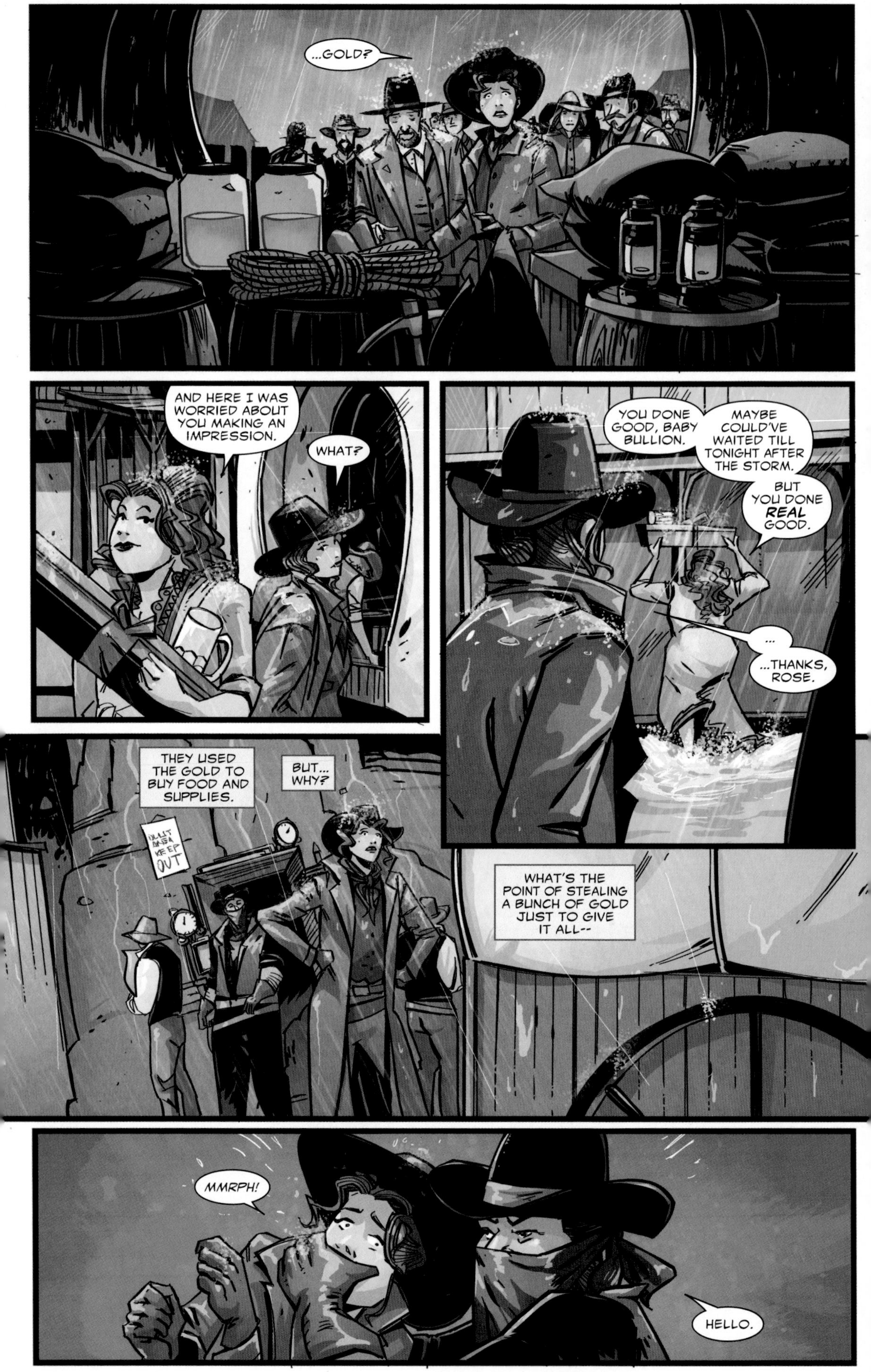
...GOLD?
AND HERE I WAS WORRIED ABOUT YOU MAKING AN IMPRESSION.
WHAT?
YOU DONE GOOD, BABY BULLION.
MAYBE COULD'VE WAITED TILL TONIGHT AFTER THE STORM.
BUT YOU DONE **REAL** GOOD.
...
...THANKS, ROSE.
THEY USED THE GOLD TO BUY FOOD AND SUPPLIES.
BUT... WHY?
WHAT'S THE POINT OF STEALING A BUNCH OF GOLD JUST TO GIVE IT ALL--
MMRPH!
HELLO.

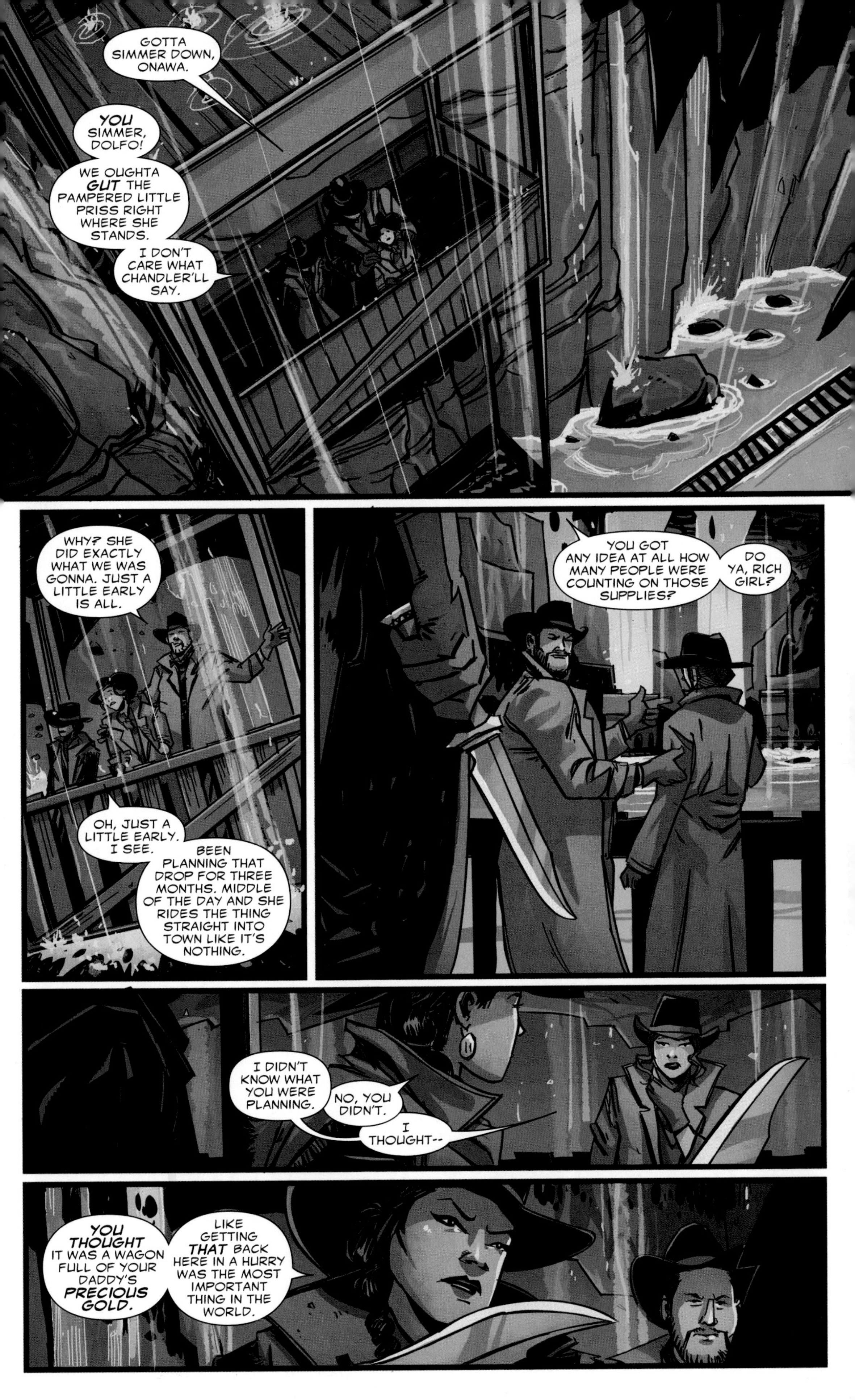
GOTTA SIMMER DOWN, ONAWA.
YOU SIMMER, DOLFO!
WE OUGHTA GUT THE PAMPERED LITTLE PRISS RIGHT WHERE SHE STANDS.
I DON'T CARE WHAT CHANDLER'LL SAY.
WHY? SHE DID EXACTLY WHAT WE WAS GONNA. JUST A LITTLE EARLY IS ALL.
OH, JUST A LITTLE EARLY. I SEE.
BEEN PLANNING THAT DROP FOR THREE MONTHS. MIDDLE OF THE DAY AND SHE RIDES THE THING STRAIGHT INTO TOWN LIKE IT'S NOTHING.
YOU GOT ANY IDEA AT ALL HOW MANY PEOPLE WERE COUNTING ON THOSE SUPPLIES?
DO YA, RICH GIRL?
I DIDN'T KNOW WHAT YOU WERE PLANNING.
NO, YOU DIDN'T.
I THOUGHT--
YOU THOUGHT IT WAS A WAGON FULL OF YOUR DADDY'S PRECIOUS GOLD.
LIKE GETTING THAT BACK HERE IN A HURRY WAS THE MOST IMPORTANT THING IN THE WORLD.

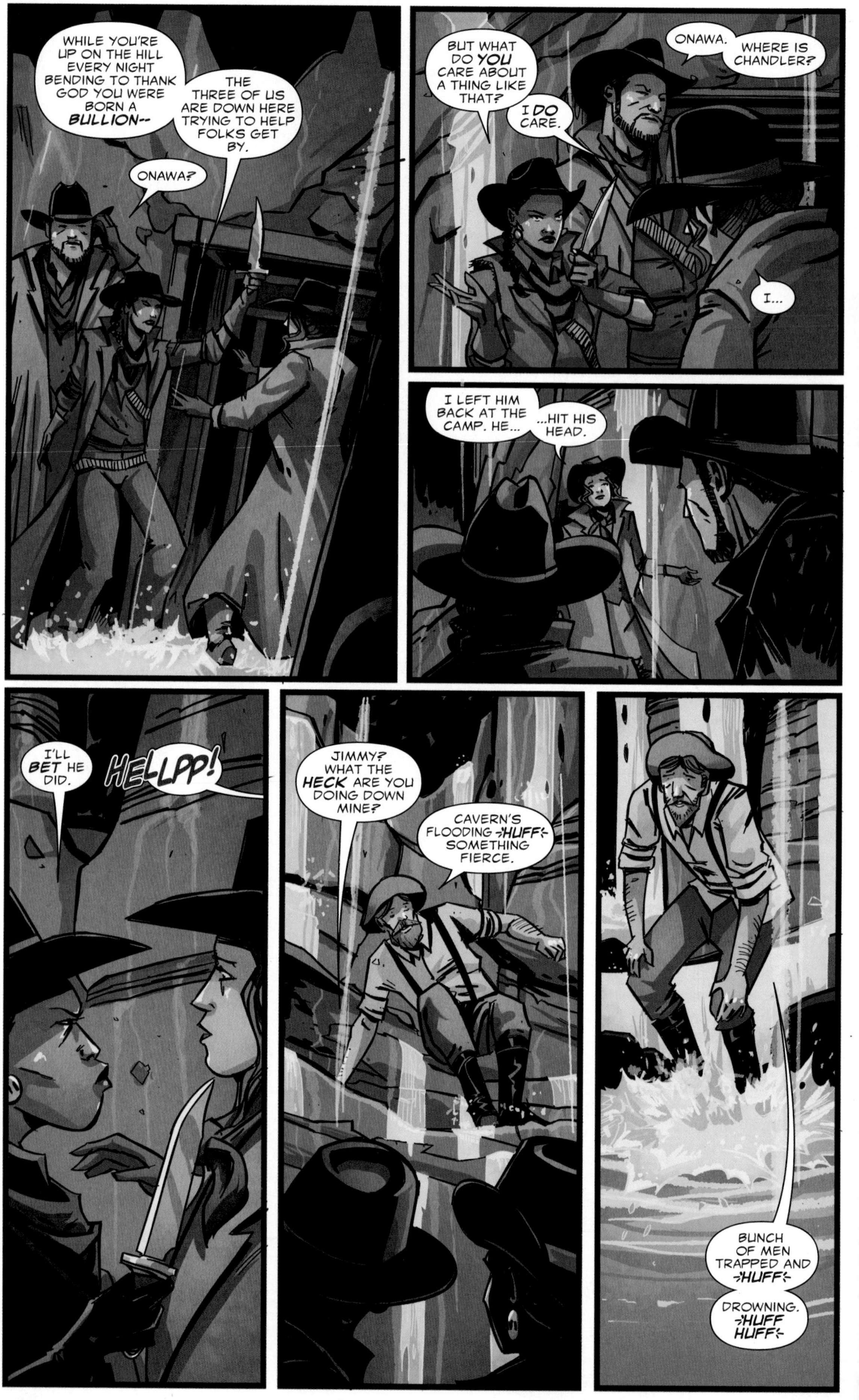
WHILE YOU'RE UP ON THE HILL EVERY NIGHT BENDING TO THANK GOD YOU WERE BORN A BULLION--
THE THREE OF US ARE DOWN HERE TRYING TO HELP FOLKS GET BY.
ONAWA?
BUT WHAT DO YOU CARE ABOUT A THING LIKE THAT?
I DO CARE.
ONAWA.
WHERE IS CHANDLER?
I...
I LEFT HIM BACK AT THE CAMP. HE...
...HIT HIS HEAD.
I'LL BET HE DID.
HELLPP!
JIMMY? WHAT THE HECK ARE YOU DOING DOWN MINE?
CAVERN'S FLOODING -HUFF- SOMETHING FIERCE.
BUNCH OF MEN TRAPPED AND -HUFF-
DROWNING. -HUFF HUFF-

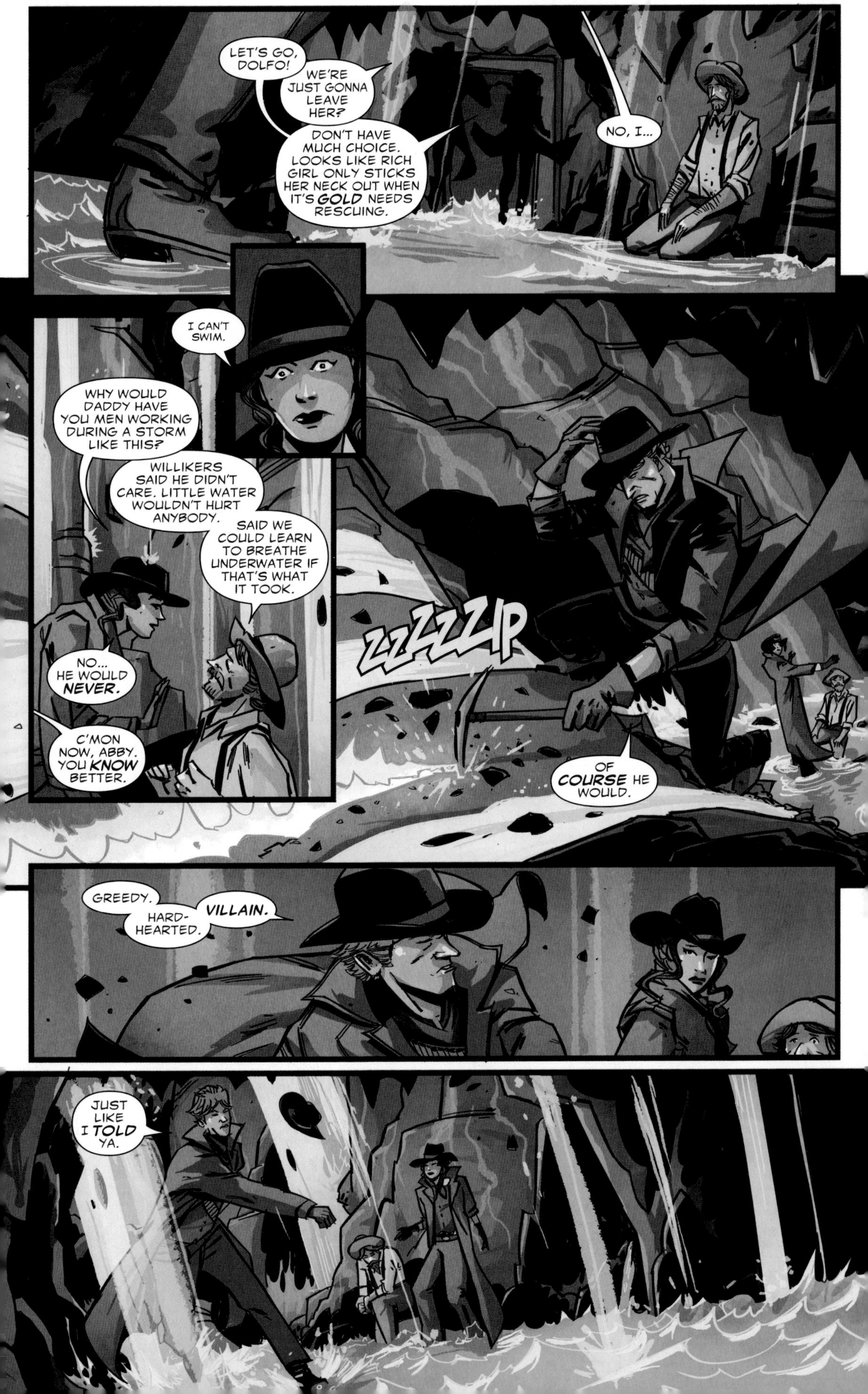
LET'S GO, DOLFO!
WE'RE JUST GONNA LEAVE HER?
DON'T HAVE MUCH CHOICE. LOOKS LIKE RICH GIRL ONLY STICKS HER NECK OUT WHEN IT'S GOLD NEEDS RESCUING.
NO, I...
I CAN'T SWIM.
WHY WOULD DADDY HAVE YOU MEN WORKING DURING A STORM LIKE THIS?
WILLIKERS SAID HE DIDN'T CARE. LITTLE WATER WOULDN'T HURT ANYBODY.
SAID WE COULD LEARN TO BREATHE UNDERWATER IF THAT'S WHAT IT TOOK.
NO... HE WOULD NEVER.
C'MON NOW, ABBY. YOU KNOW BETTER.
ZZZZZIP
OF COURSE HE WOULD.
GREEDY.
HARD-HEARTED.
VILLAIN.
JUST LIKE I TOLD YA.

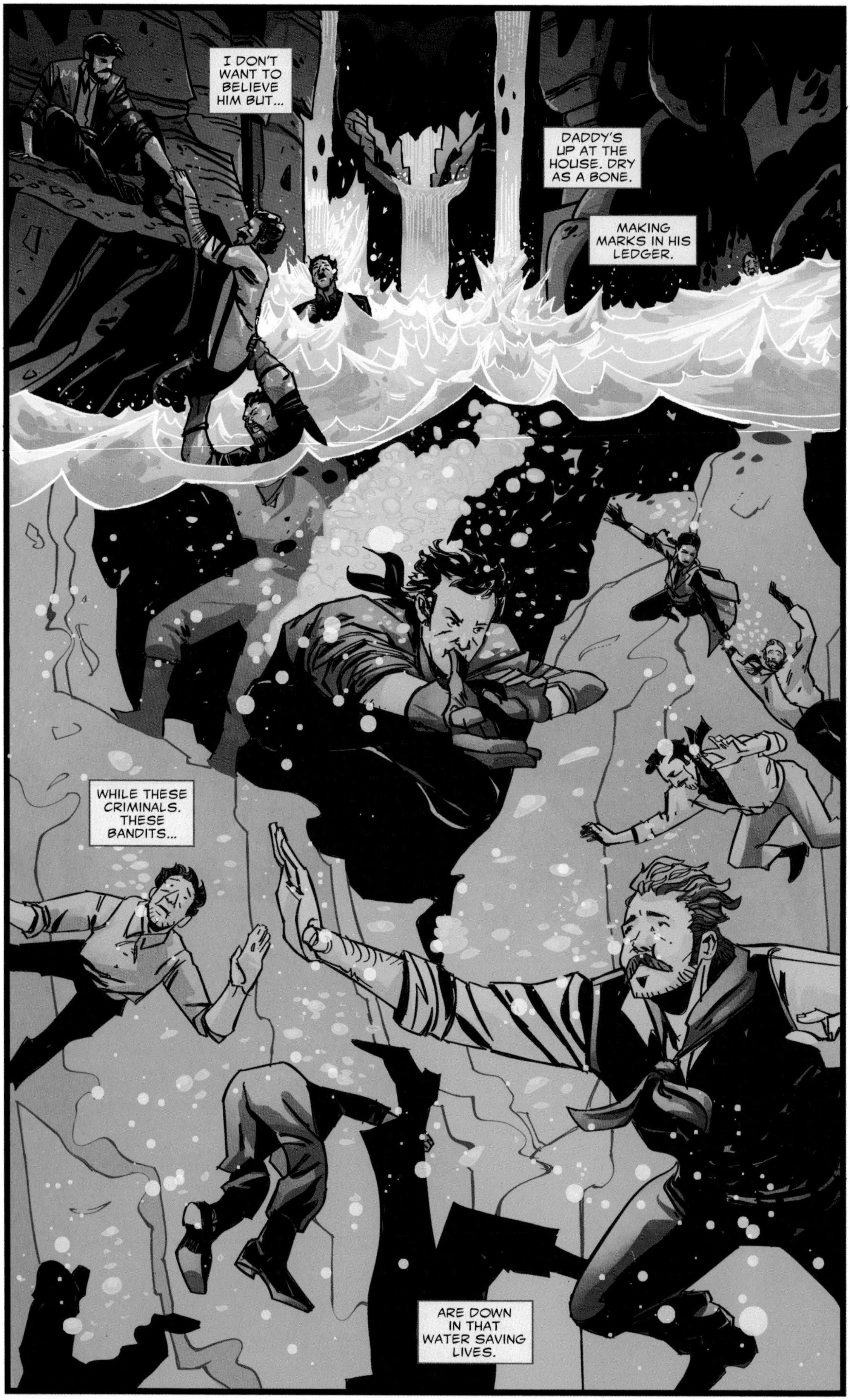
I DON'T WANT TO BELIEVE HIM BUT...
DADDY'S UP AT THE HOUSE. DRY AS A BONE.
MAKING MARKS IN HIS LEDGER.
WHILE THESE CRIMINALS. THESE BANDITS...
ARE DOWN IN THAT WATER SAVING LIVES.

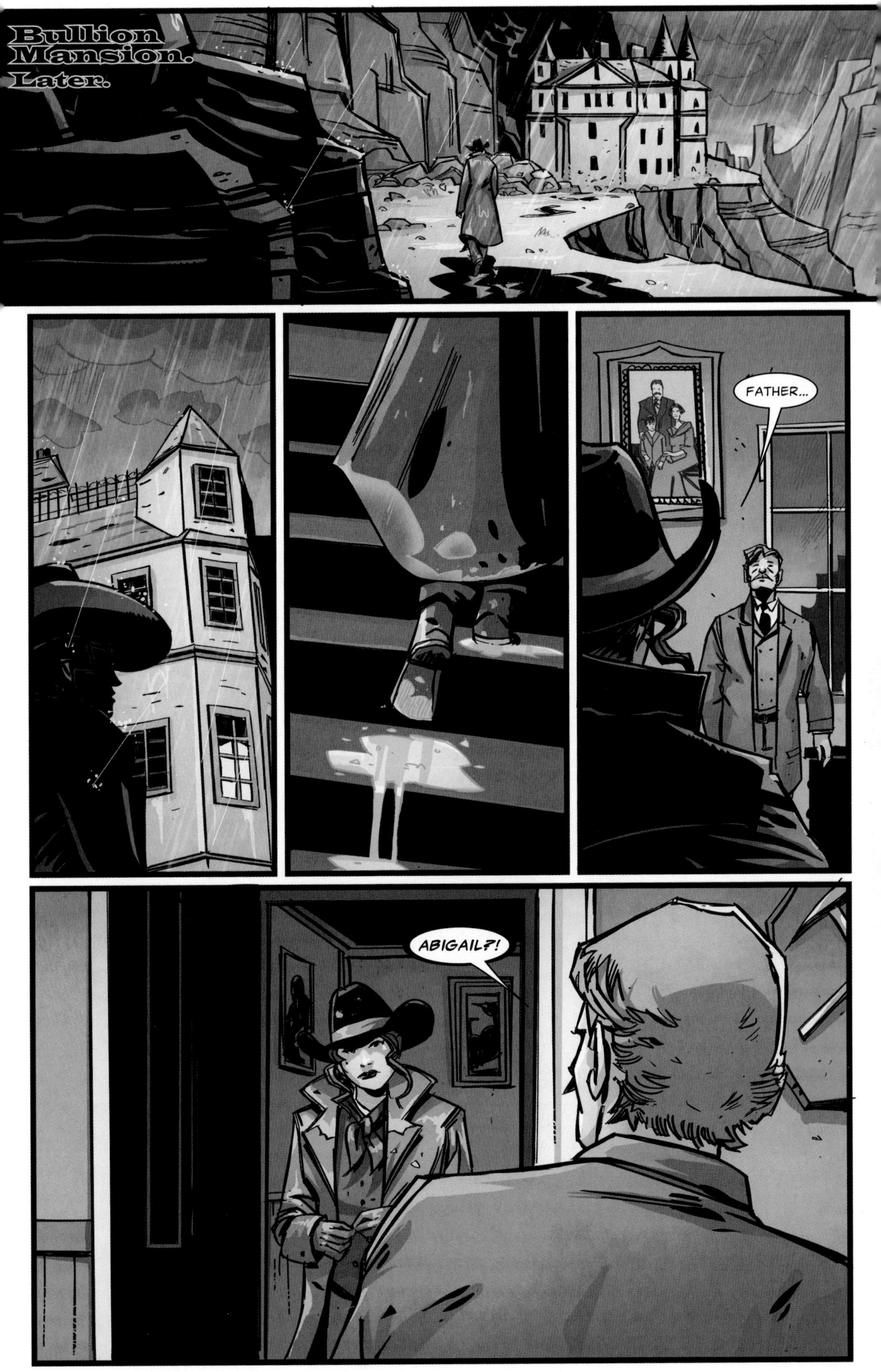
Bullion Mansion. Later.
FATHER...
ABIGAIL?!

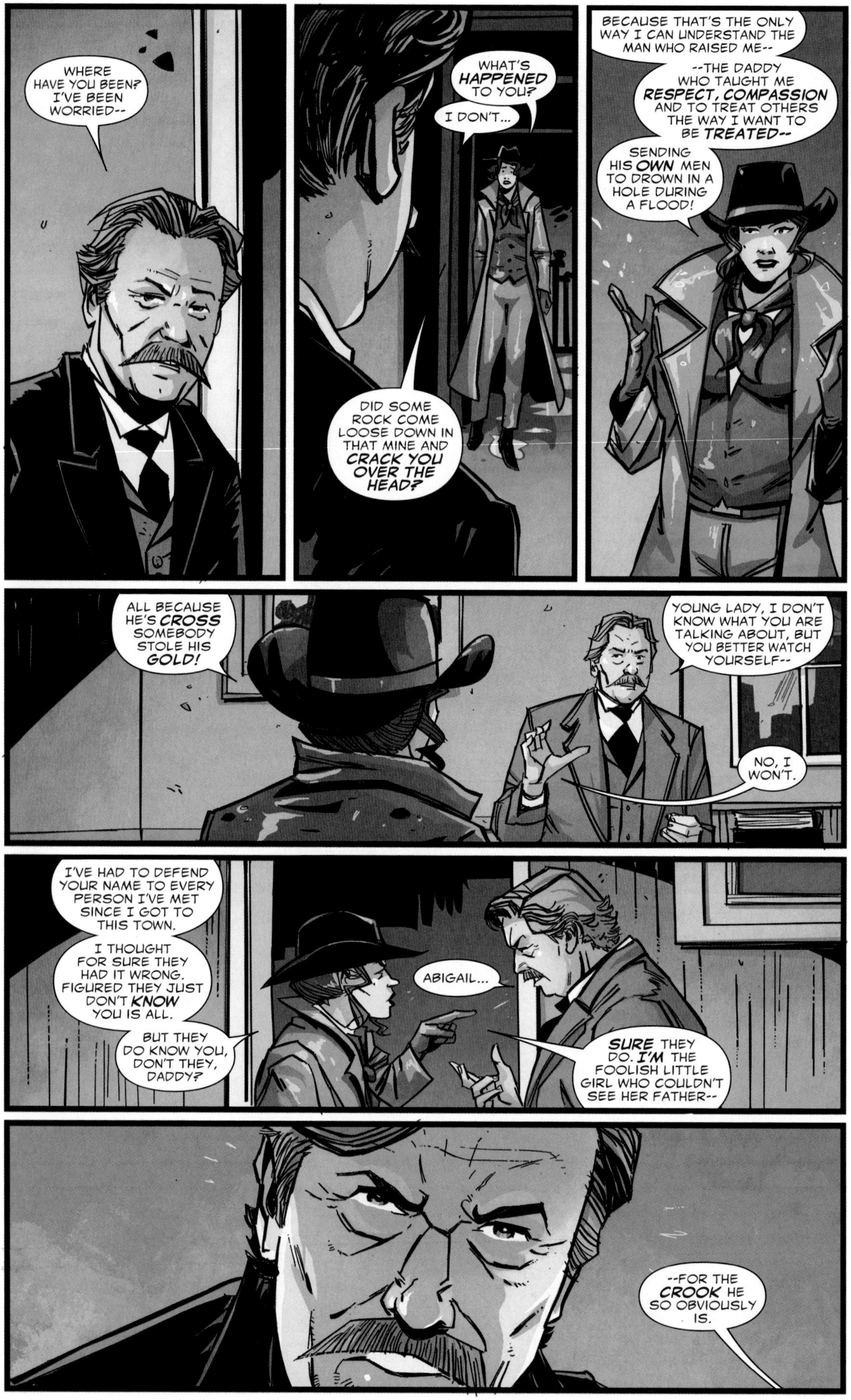
WHERE HAVE YOU BEEN? I'VE BEEN WORRIED--
WHAT'S HAPPENED TO YOU?
I DON'T...
DID SOME ROCK COME LOOSE DOWN IN THAT MINE AND CRACK YOU OVER THE HEAD?
BECAUSE THAT'S THE ONLY WAY I CAN UNDERSTAND THE MAN WHO RAISED ME--
--THE DADDY WHO TAUGHT ME RESPECT, COMPASSION AND TO TREAT OTHERS THE WAY I WANT TO BE TREATED--
SENDING HIS OWN MEN TO DROWN IN A HOLE DURING A FLOOD!
ALL BECAUSE HE'S CROSS SOMEBODY STOLE HIS GOLD!
YOUNG LADY, I DON'T KNOW WHAT YOU ARE TALKING ABOUT, BUT YOU BETTER WATCH YOURSELF--
NO, I WON'T.
I'VE HAD TO DEFEND YOUR NAME TO EVERY PERSON I'VE MET SINCE I GOT TO THIS TOWN.
I THOUGHT FOR SURE THEY HAD IT WRONG. FIGURED THEY JUST DON'T KNOW YOU IS ALL.
BUT THEY DO KNOW YOU, DON'T THEY, DADDY?
ABIGAIL...
SURE THEY DO. I'M THE FOOLISH LITTLE GIRL WHO COULDN'T SEE HER FATHER--
--FOR THE CROOK HE SO OBVIOUSLY IS.

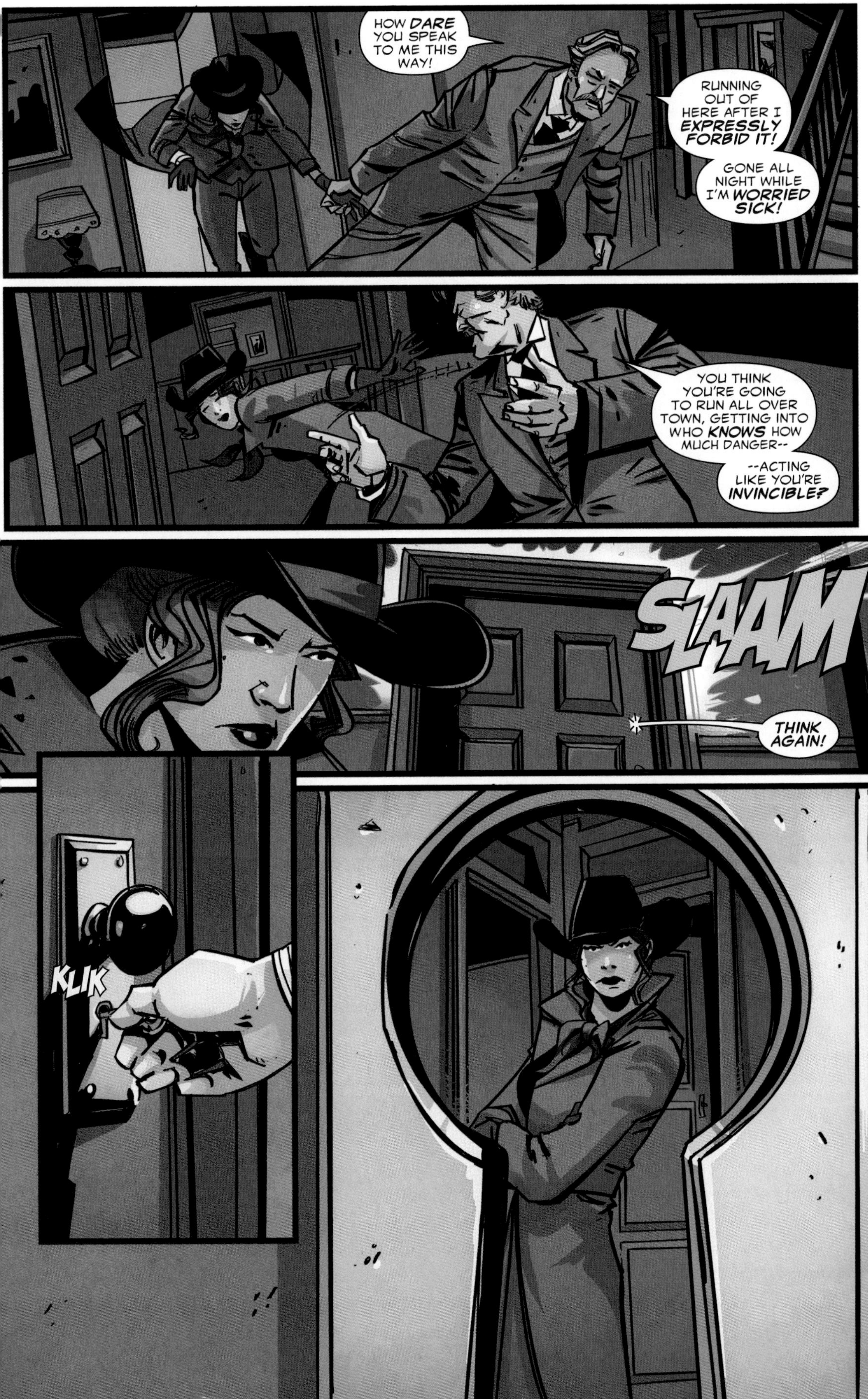
HOW DARE YOU SPEAK TO ME THIS WAY!
RUNNING OUT OF HERE AFTER I EXPRESSLY FORBID IT!
GONE ALL NIGHT WHILE I'M WORRIED SICK!
YOU THINK YOU'RE GOING TO RUN ALL OVER TOWN, GETTING INTO WHO KNOWS HOW MUCH DANGER--
--ACTING LIKE YOU'RE INVINCIBLE?
SLAAM
THINK AGAIN!
KLIK

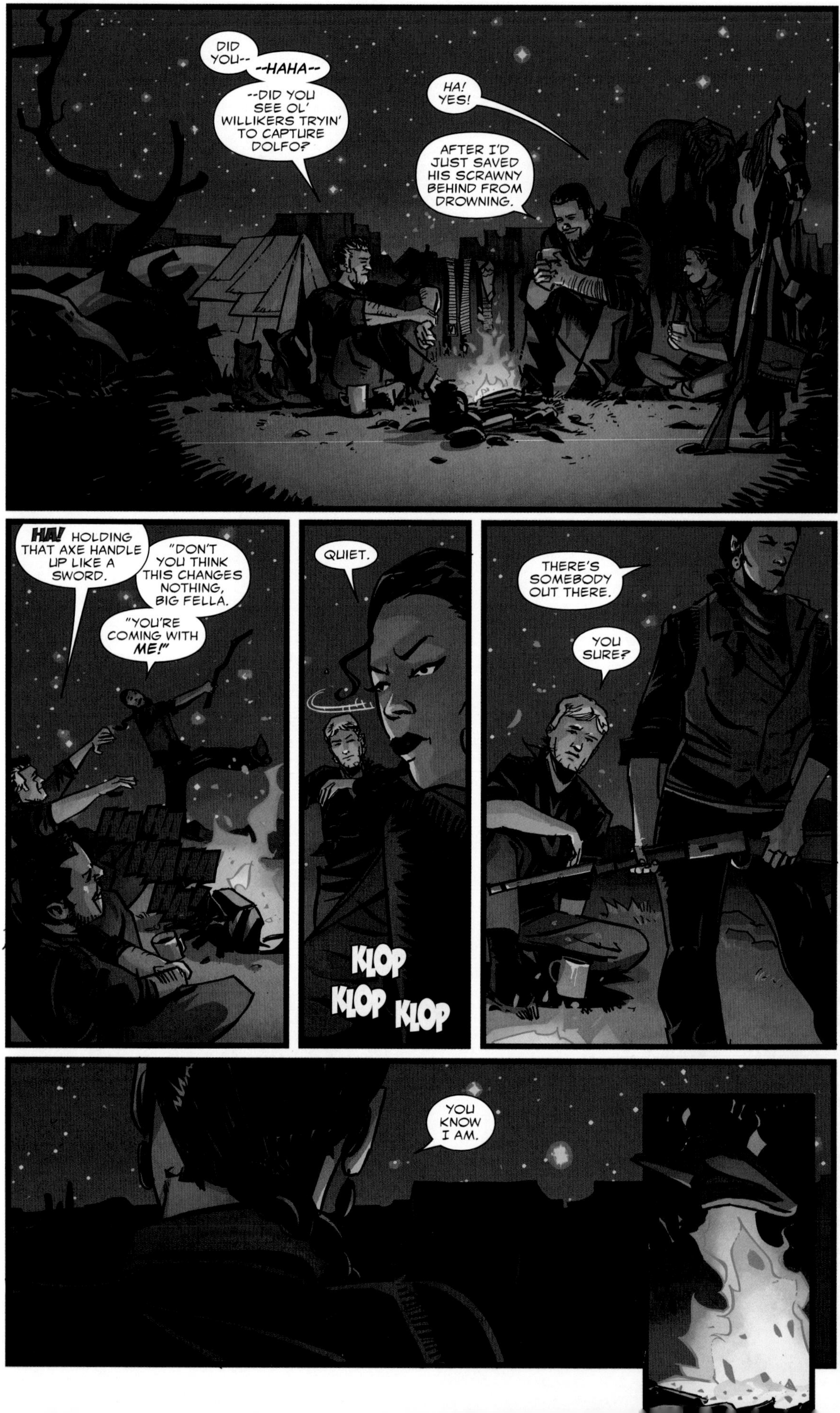
DID YOU--
--HAHA--
--DID YOU SEE OL' WILLIKERS TRYIN' TO CAPTURE DOLFO?
HA! YES!
AFTER I'D JUST SAVED HIS SCRAWNY BEHIND FROM DROWNING.
HA! HOLDING THAT AXE HANDLE UP LIKE A SWORD.
"DON'T YOU THINK THIS CHANGES NOTHING, BIG FELLA.
"YOU'RE COMING WITH ME!"
QUIET.
KLOP
KLOP KLOP
THERE'S SOMEBODY OUT THERE.
YOU SURE?
YOU KNOW I AM.

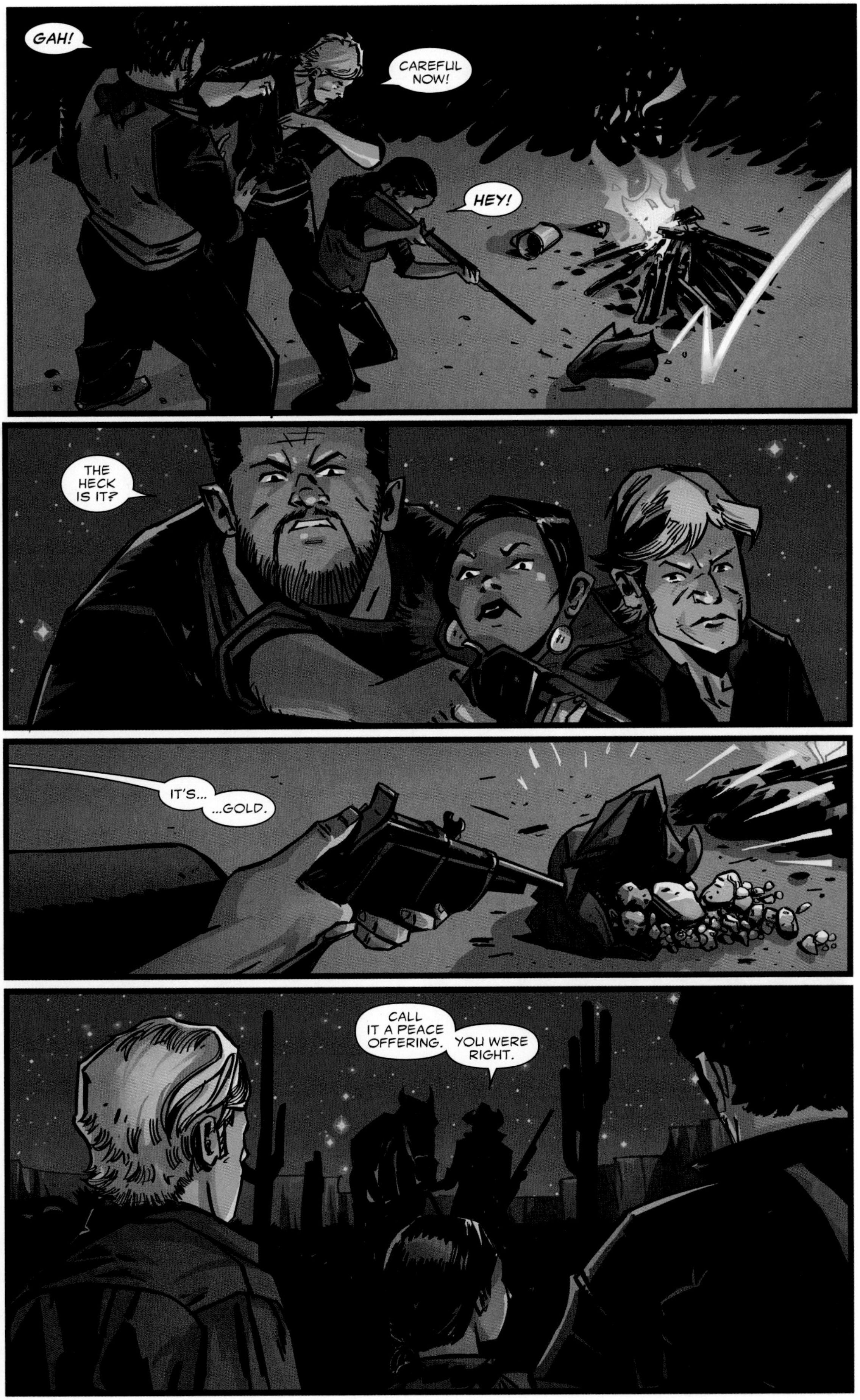
GAH!
CAREFUL NOW!
HEY!
THE HECK IS IT?
IT'S...
...GOLD.
CALL IT A PEACE OFFERING.
YOU WERE RIGHT.

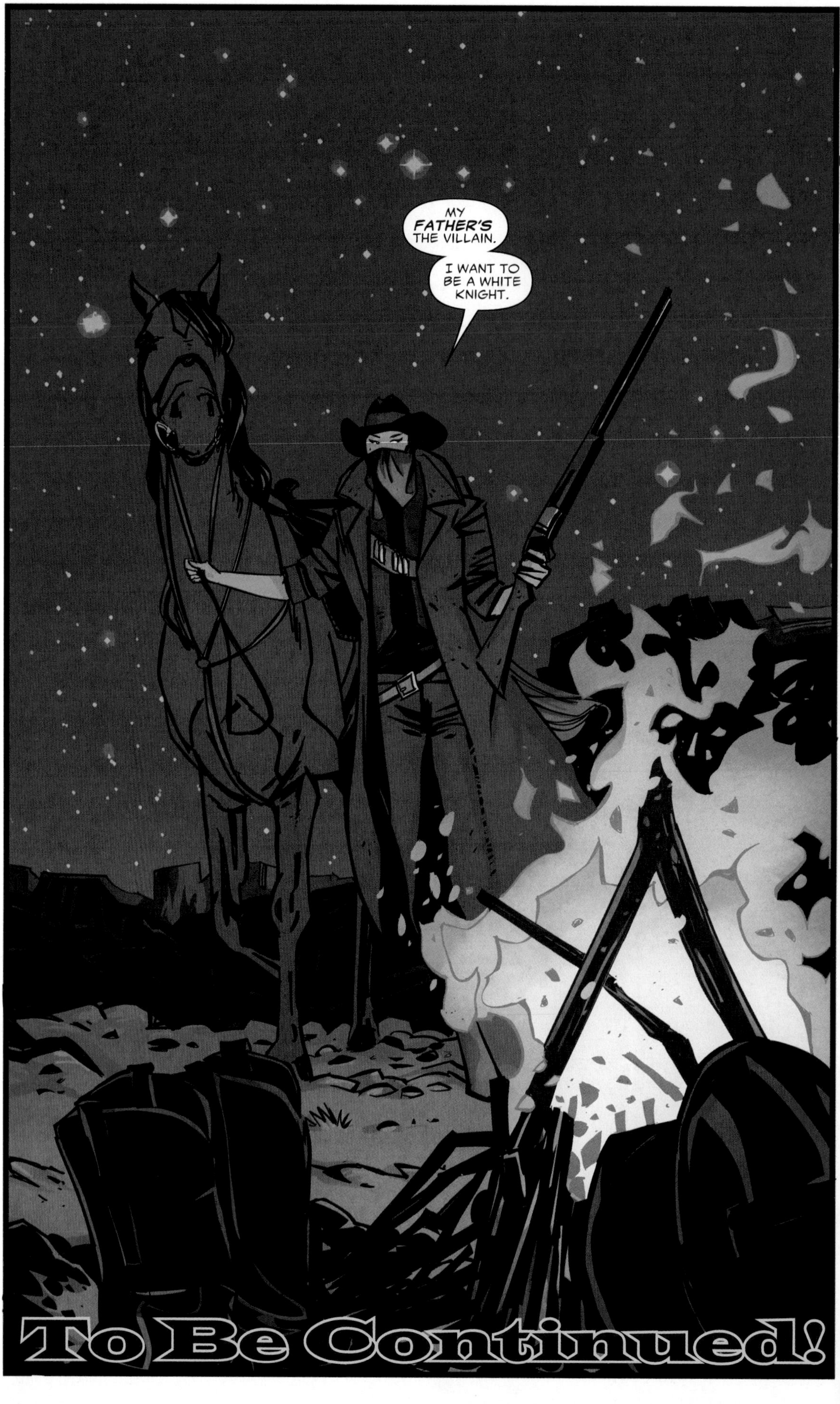

MY FATHER'S THE VILLAIN.
I WANT TO BE A WHITE KNIGHT.
To Be Continued!

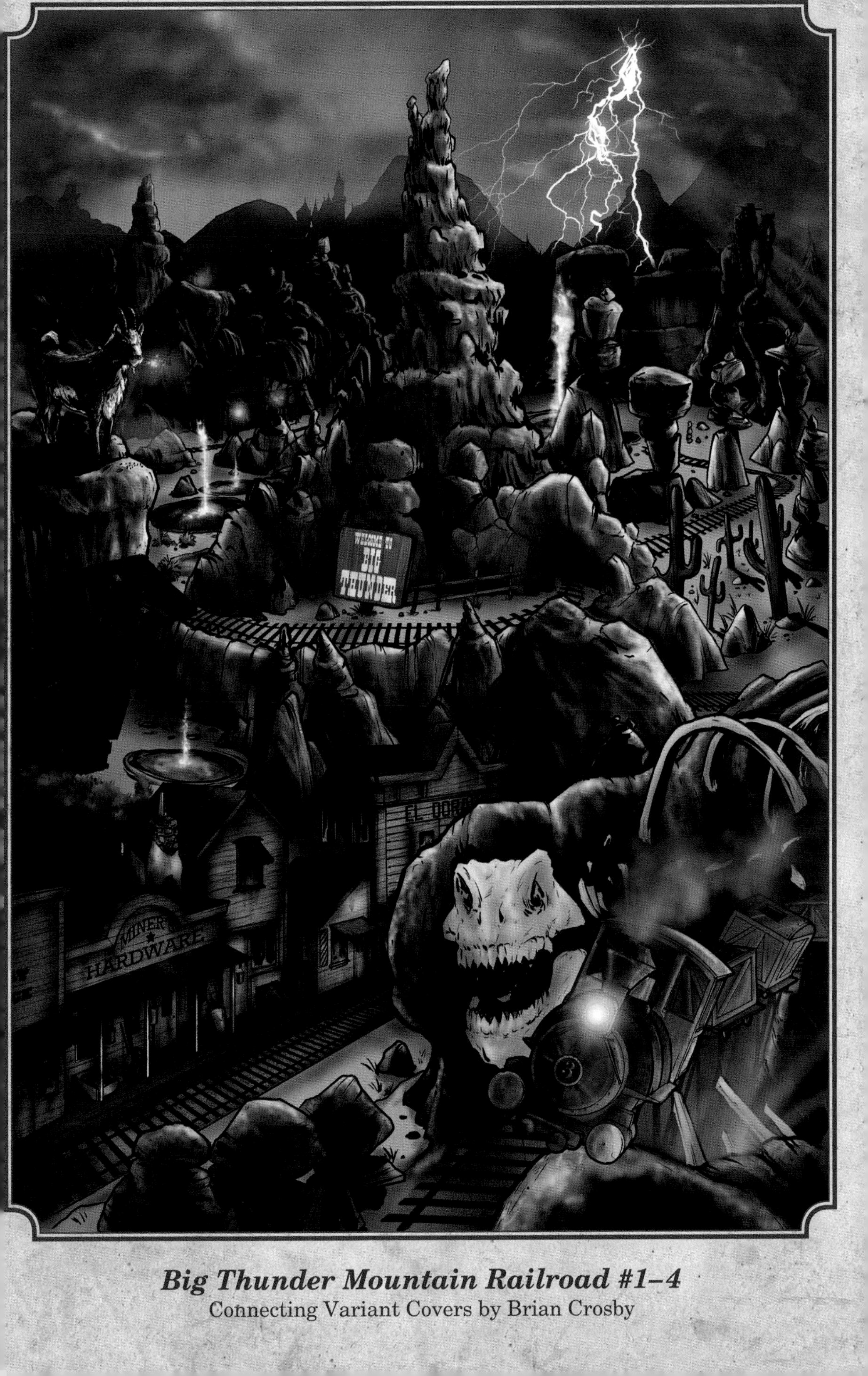
WELCOME TO
BIG
THUNDER
EL DORA
MINER
HARDWARE

Big Thunder Mountain Railroad #1–4
Connecting Variant Covers by Brian Crosby

Hardcover Book ISBN
978-1-61479-575-9

COLLECT
THEM
ALL!

Set of 5
Hardcover Books ISBN:
978-1-61479-574-2

Hardcover Book ISBN
978-1-61479-576-6

Hardcover Book ISBN
978-1-61479-577-3

Hardcover Book ISBN
978-1-61479-578-0

Hardcover Book ISBN
978-1-61479-579-7